Inspiring Women
to Take a Closer Look

Angela Dixon

Entegrity Choice Publishing
PO Box 453
Powder Springs, GA 30127
info@entegritypublishing.com
www.entegritypublishing.com
770.727.6517

Printed in the United States of America

Library of Congress Cataloging-in-Publication Data
ISBN 978-1-7330301-8-2
Library of Congress Control Number: 2020903338

Contents

Dedication

This book is written and dedicated to countless women who are seeking God's true design for marriage. If that is you, this book seeks to awaken a desire to view marriage according to God's word and will.

I would like to thank God for my parents Frank and Delores who are both now deceased. I did not grow up in a Christian home, but I am especially grateful for my mom, because she introduced me to my first church at age 12. I met God there and His son Jesus on a personal level.

A shout out to my Siblings; Glenda, Joycelyn, Victoria, Leonard, Elston, Frank Jr and Terry. A shout-out to my youngest brother, Terry, who would always say, "You know your book." And to my oldest brother, Leonard, who would always ask me, "How's it going?"

To my grandmother, Edna, who is also deceased: Although I don't remember very much about her, I do recall some Sunday mornings when she would sit on the couch watching *The Jubilee Showcase*. As I sat on the floor between her legs, she always draped her hands over my face, and I had to look between her fingers to watch this gospel program filled with songs. Although it was somewhat hard for me to watch the program, I remember the feeling of peace when I listened as different artists sang those old hymns. I see how God used my grandmother to introduce me to spiritual music and how His hand was on my life as a child.

To Jacqueline Sweetpea Calhoun—my Co-Editor, cousin, sister in Christ, and friend: Thank you so much. I love you.

To Evelyn, a friend for life: Thank you for always having a listening ear.

To Wanda my spiritual mentor in Christ, thanks for speaking the truth even when it hurt. And to my dear friend Teresa, I thank God for you.

To the Apostles, Prophets, Evangelists, Teachers, and Pastors that have spoken into and over my life: I truly do thank and praise God for your labor of love. Thank you so much with love.

To my beautiful children, Keith, Alecia, Angel, Kevin and Raymond: In my failures and mistakes as a parent, I have learned so much from you all. I want to thank you for putting up with me, especially during those times you did not always get the best out of me. You somehow would always manage to see the best in me.

Last, but not least, to the little loves of my life—Josiah and J'Nya: Nene loves you. And to my newest grandchild on the way: Nene looks forward to meeting you.

Introduction

I thank God, through his son Jesus Christ, for giving me the opportunity to write this book. It has given me a platform to share some of my uncomfortable, difficult, and painful experiences that are now overcoming testimonies. Through them, I gained the Godly wisdom, knowledge, and understanding that He is now able to use for His glory.

The purpose of this book is to inspire women of all ages to take a closer look at the vows of marriage, and ask themselves one question: Why am I getting married?

Answering this question will help you to look beneath the surface of a man's outward exterior. This discovery will, in turn, keep you from being guided by your emotions alone. You will also learn that emotions do not discriminate, that they play important roles in our lives, and that they are pitfalls when we are solely led by them.

Most women of the household of faith understand that God is the One who instituted marriage, and that the vows recited during a ceremony are spoken to Him. Therefore, if or when a mate is presented, this understanding should cause you to make the right choice when deciding if you should accept the proposal of marriage.

Marriage is a ministry, and when accepting a proposal, we need to see beyond a male's natural talents, possessions, gifts, and abilities, in order to see the spiritual man inside.

One of the main focuses of this book is about making right choices. God wants women to understand that there is so much more to relationships than what we see on the surface, and He wants us to understand just how real they are. Our relationships with parents, relatives, our children, siblings, and friends have either left positive or negative effects in our lives. The effects of each encounter did not go away when adulthood was reached, but they were carried from one relationship to the next.

Author's Note

In writing this book, *Inspiring Women to Take a Closer Look,* I want to stress that I still believe in God's divine order for marriage. This includes the principle that a woman is not to exert authority over the man, because God has appointed him as head priest over the home. However, I do believe it is important to marry the right man. Also, I want to call your attention to the value God has placed in you, and the value you bring to the union of marriage and relationships.

1

Preparations Before the Vows

REQUEST THE HONOR OF YOUR PRESENCE
AT THE MARRIAGE OF THEIR DAUGHTER

Mr. & Mrs.

SATURDAY, THE TWELFTH OF MAY
TWO THOUSAND EIGHTEEN
AT HALF AFTER SIX IN THE EVENING

ST. MARY'S CATHOLIC CHURCH
1451 OLD SHELL ROAD
MOBILE, ALABAMA

Table
Table
Table
Table
1
2
3
4
G
H
This is whe

2

Why Do I Want to Get Married?

Regardless of age, this is a very important question. The answer will determine what a woman will allow in her life, and what will be brought to the lives of those in her close circle. It really does matter to God how people view the marriage union. A spontaneous decision to marry can cause one to deviate from his purpose, thereby nullifying and making His plan for life ineffective.

Because of the way we were designed by God, it is in our nature to want a mate. *"He created them male and female, and He blessed them and called them human." Genesis 5:2 NLT.* Eve was formed from a rib taken out of Adam.

"At last! The man exclaimed, This one is bone from my bone, and flesh from my flesh! She will be called woman, because she was taken out of man."
Genesis 2:23 NLT

We sometimes see toddlers showing affectionate desire in early stages of life. Do you remember playing house as a little girl? There was always a mom, a dad, and of course the baby. Even then, we were operating from a desire that was naturally instilled in us by our Creator.

When single, most of us hope that Prince Charming or a knight in shining armor will come and sweep us off our feet, as we ride away in the sun to live happily ever after. Sometimes, when we are anticipating marriage, we want the fairy tale wedding, and for some, this does come to pass. These desires are evidence that God was preparing us for the future life of the ministry of marriage and children. He has a way of molding, making, and shaping us, without us knowing His awesome plan for our lives.

Does marriage and having children define us?

Certainly not! They are just a beauty within themselves.

But no matter how and why God decides to release His blessing, we can all agree that IT IS GOOD!

"Then God looked over all he had made, and He saw that it was very good!"
Genesis 1:31 NLT

We love His infinite wisdom, and how He knows all things. Jesus Himself said, *"And the very hairs on your head are all numbered."* Matthew 10:30 NLT

When in a relationship, we have desires. We want it to last; we want to be the apple of his eye, to be told we are beautiful, and much more. This only names a few, but I am sure that as you ponder, you can add some of your own.

Desire plays a big part in our emotions too, and while it's ok to have these desires, we need to know who gave them to us or where they come from. Desire comes from God. Therefore, it becomes necessary that we depend on Him to help us manage our desire and our emotions, before we make lifelong commitments.

Why is it necessary to depend on God in this way? I am glad you asked! Since desire came from God, I believe there is a spark built in our human nature that naturally sets off a desire for companionship. That spark is connected directly to our emotions, making us vulnerable, overly anxious, and even causing us to act desperate at times, if we don't depend on God to help us. This can be especially true if we feel our biological clock ticking, and we haven't accomplished our goals. We could potentially become so preoccupied and filled with distress, that it erupts into a state of worry.

> *"Don't worry about anything; instead pray, about everything. Tell God what you need and thank Him for all He has done."*
> *Philippians 4:6 NLT*

First and foremost, God loves us so much. He does not want us to be anxious for anything, because He knows worry is not good for us. We are instructed to present our requests, for this purpose.

This will allow us to learn His will as it pertains to our care.

> **"Give all your worries and cares to God,**
> **for He cares about you."**
> **1 Peter 5:7 NLT**

God wants us to know that our desires are ultimately His desires for us. He just helps us to want, for ourselves, the very things He wants for us.

It was such a delight, when I learned that God wants us to have a choice, and that we can ask Him for what we want, when it comes to choosing a mate. I believe, when we are fully persuaded about who we are, and Whom we belong to, we will at no point settle for less than God's best; and His best is whomever He has for you. This does not mean he will be perfect, but he will be the best for you.

As you continue reading, my hope is that we all arrive at the same conclusion: that it's not just enough to have a man. The question becomes, "Is he the God-sent man?"

Marriage Vows

"I, ___, take thee, ___, to be my wedded husband/ wife, to have and to hold, from this day forward, for better, for worse, for richer, for poorer, in sickness and in health, to love and to cherish, till death do us part, according to God's holy ordinance; and thereto I pledge thee my faith [or] pledge myself to you."

3
Is He Willing?

Is he ready? He may not be fully developed for marriage, and that's ok, because we're not either. But having a genuine heart that is after God's heart, makes him pliable in the Potter's hands. His aim will not be just to please himself, but to please God and you. He will seek a vision for his family, accepting his role as head priest over his home, and not as the blocker of the blessing.

*"In the same way, you husbands must give honor
to your wives. Treat your wife with understanding, as you live together. She may be weaker than
you are, but she is your equal partner in God's
gift of new life. Treat her as you should,
so your prayers will not be hindered."
1 Peter 3:7 NLT*

Spoken in simple terms, God says, "Guys, let me help you out! Here I am, an all-knowing God. I can make it easier for you."

As the husband is willing, God will teach him how to allow his wife's beautiful attributes to flow. Established boundaries will allow her to go forward in her own individual ministry, in whatever way God sees fit to use her in the body of Christ. This husband is not threatened or intimidated by her calling, and because of his reverence for God, he will not interfere with her assignment.

> **"A wise woman builds her home, but a foolish woman tears it down with her own hands."**
> **Proverbs 14:1 NLT**

If we don't allow God to help us with making right choices, then we choose to go our own way. God's mercy is there on our behalf. He can and will get the glory, but doing things our own way is like going the long way around and can be very painful. Some of us are like the children of Israel. Their time of captivity in Egypt was not by choice. However, by doing things their own way after God delivered them out of Egypt, they became captive by their own choices.

God does not force us to make the right choice when we're presented with decisions, but if we ask, He'll help us to do what's right. In the Garden of Eden, Adam had a will, but God gave him a command. *"But the Lord God, warned him, you may freely eat the fruit of every tree in the garden, except the tree of the knowledge of good and evil. If you eat its fruit, you are sure to die." Genesis 2:16-17 NLT*

In the next paragraphs, we talk about how imperative it is that a chosen mate remain pliable in God's hand. Differences and opinions are the key source of dilemmas, conflicts, and confusion.

Our words form opinions, and our opinions form our views. This makes it difficult and sometimes impossible for us to reach a common ground where we can see eye to eye. The opinions we can't manage create undesirable emotions that can spiral out of control. Emotions and desires are different between male and female. While God has given men emotions, they are certainly not like ours. But they do have them. Sometimes we wonder. **Really?**

I think, men and women are wired similarly, in some ways. However, there are some differences which make the way we process information different. I certainly do thank and appreciate God for the man, and it all does make sense. I can imagine God saying it like this, "They would be totally out of balance if they were both emotional roller coasters at the same time."

I have heard that women are the emotional side of the man. Is there truth in this statement? Hmmm… I know, we do have a way of bringing them in touch with their emotional side. I am going somewhere with this, so stay with me.

> *"Then the Lord God said, it is not good*
> *for the man to be alone. I will make a helper,*
> *who is just right for him."*
> **Genesis 2:18 NLT**

Then He went to work on her, making it a union.

*"Then the Lord God made a woman from the rib,
and He brought her to the man."*
Genesis 2:22 NLT

Satan's number one priority is to divide the union of marriage established by God. After Adam fell, it not only separated us from God, but it also separated us from one another.

*"Your desire will be for your husband,
and he will rule over you."*
Genesis 3:16 NIV

I have such a high admiration for God, because despite all of Satan's attempts, God works circles around the devil and his schemes. I marvel at that.

Because of God having to go another way after the fall, he put another one of his brilliant plans into action to get us back to a form of Eden. *"I'm declaring war between you and the Woman, between your offspring and hers."* Genesis 3:15 MSG

God made it where we needed to come into agreement with Him. Previously, Adam and Eve had agreed together with the devil. It was wrong, but they did agree.

*"The woman was convinced.
She saw that the tree was beautiful,
and its fruit looked delicious, and she wanted the
wisdom it would give her. So, she took some of the
fruit and ate it. Then she gave some to her husband, who was with her, and he ate it, too."*
Genesis 3:6 NLT

It's a method not to be excluded, as it relates to the body of Christ, and it will work in relationships on all terms. It's called the power of agreement.

> ***"'Look he said. The people are united, and they all speak the same language. After this, nothing they set out to do will be impossible for them."***
> ***Genesis 11:6 NLT***

The enemy fights relationships at all cost, because he understands this power. Satan is well organized, and it does him a service if we choose to remain ignorant by continually walking in darkness. He uses many tactics, but his chief strategies are to deceive, conquer, and divide.

> ***"If a house is divided against itself, that house cannot stand."***
> ***Mark 3:25 NIV***

Whenever the devil is working to keep one spouse in opposition of the other, if that individual chooses opposition, he or she is willingly operating from a rebellious stance. That person then becomes unwilling to yield to the will of God. Let's see how Abraham responded to God's will concerning Ishmael and Isaac.

> ***"But Sarah saw Ishmael—the son of Abraham and her Egyptian servant Hagar—making fun of her son, Isaac. So she turned to Abraham and demanded, Get rid of that slave woman and her son. He is not going to share the inheritance with my son, Isaac. I won't have it! This upset Abraham***

very much because Ishmael was his son. But God told Abraham, Do not be upset over the boy and your servant. Do whatever Sarah tells you, for Isaac is the son through whom your descendants will be counted. But I will also make a nation of the descendants of Hagar's son because he is your son, too. So Abraham got up early the next morning, prepared food and a container of water, and strapped them on Hagar's shoulders. Then he sent her away with their son."
Genesis 21:9-14a NLT

When the husband tells the wife she is nagging, that is another one of Satan schemes. It allows the husband to take the easy way out, and allows him to avoid all acts of showing interest in unresolved problems. Now, ladies, we certainly don't want to make excuses for our shortcomings. We know how difficult we can become, when we are in our demanding moments.

"It is better to dwell in a corner of the housetop, than with a brawling woman in a wide house."
Proverbs 21:9

I have come to believe that there are some things a man will never gain insight into, that God has designed to come specifically through a woman. It's not that He cannot use anyone else, but God intended for us to have relationships involving submission and respect.

"Can two walk together, except they be agreed?"
Amos 3:3

4
Let's Go on
an Imaginary Journey

This journey of imagination is not to be mis-interpreted. It is not intended to mislead or incite any form of regret on behalf of any child or parent. We are exploring the essentials needed to prevent worst-case scenarios.

Sometimes, women bring children into negative environments which lack the fundamentals needed for life. These environments are not conducive to instilling proper standards, values, and beliefs in them. Have you heard the saying, "Child, where is your mama?"

The impact of such negative choices affects the lives of so many children, and we see it daily. They are coming from unstructured and broken homes, but God still has a plan to instill family values in them. A chosen mate should possess qualities for positive and Godly influence. Actually, when we marry, we gain another set of views on how we are to do things. We must not allow our children to be the generation that knew not God.

> ***"And also, all that generation were gathered unto their fathers: and there arose another generation after them, which knew not the Lord, nor yet the works which he had done for Israel."***
> ***Judges 2:10***

Let the journey begin! Imagine that you've done what you wanted to do, and you're married now. You find yourself unequally yoked; you were so from the beginning. He can be in or out of the church, have a relationship with God, or not. Just in case you didn't know—and this may come as a surprise—but you can be right in the church and be unequally yoked with a believer.

Think about these scenarios:

1. What if you've given birth to your first baby? You both work opposite shifts, and when baby is left in his care, he doesn't cease from drinking to the point of intoxication. His habit was clearly made known to you before the marriage, and he has kept this same habit after the marriage.

2. Imagine you are trying to instill the importance of educational values in your

children. Your mate is very much aware of your standards, values, and beliefs, however, his actions go against these principals. For example, he goes against your principles by allowing them to watch videos. In Mark 3:25, Jesus said, *"If a house be divided against itself, that house cannot stand."* Then the question, in your home, becomes, "Who will set the standards?"

3. Let's say, you meet a man who has class and possesses qualities and attributes you desire. You find yourself physically attracted to him, and (let's keep it real) you have been waiting awhile. He has his own business, he is financially well off, generous, and loves to travel. If it sounds too good to be true, it's not; they are out there. As you get to know this man, our God, who is always demonstrating his love for us, shows you that this man has old traditions instilled inside his heart. His beliefs are that women are not to have a voice or question him. Now we know this goes beneath the surface without a shadow of any doubt, and it is at that very moment we are challenged with a choice.

Here are some things we tell ourselves when we want to make the shoe fit: I can change him, I can tolerate it, I can pray him through. We spend so much time dancing with the devil, instead of asking the Holy Spirit to guide us, or instead of obeying the Word.

I will be transparent here and share an experience that I had. At times, I still find it hard to forgive myself for all that happened. I found myself in the worst relationship ever. I was driven by loneliness, attraction, and a desire for companionship.

I was led away with a desire. We called it 'quality time.' This is something I considered important in any relationship—turning off the phone, gazing into each other's eyes, totally shutting off the outside world, having each other's undivided attention. He was tall, and yes, indeed, he was dark and handsome. He could put on a blue shirt and make your head swim. At least he made my head swim.

He always made me feel like Cinderella. The only thing missing was the big dress. I was certain that my guy knew he had one of God's jewels. But you can have a jewel and not know its true value.

After attending service on Sunday morning, as I would step down from the curb, he would extend his hand as if he never wanted me to fall. Yet, there were red flags, and one of them was signs of anger. I continued to find ways to say this relationship was good for me, even after his outbursts of anger began to surface.

I was not allowing God to really help me. My emotions had become very much involved. No, my attachment was not sexual, because for the first time, I learned intimacy outside of sex. It's not that I didn't want to engage sexually, but instead I reveled in how curious he appeared to be about my personality as a woman. I want to make my boast only in the Lord, and proudly say, God kept me from becoming sexually involved. I know Him to be a Keeper, and He can keep us even as we make painful decisions. This man was feeding my God-given desire to be a woman and to be loved.

During this time, I was certainly distracted, but I am grateful that communication with God was not totally lost. God began showing me more horrible things that were etched in this man's soul. He became hostile, but God restrained him. Can you believe I was still making excuses? I continued talking to God in my alone time, and my heart was crying out to Him. I was thankful that there was still a desire of only wanting what was right for me.

I felt strongly about leaving the relationship so that I would no longer be compromising my spiritual, emotional, and mental well-being. After having endured a failed marriage of twenty-one years, I am all-too-familiar with the relentless hours it took in prayer and the Word of God, to restore me to who I am today!

This phrase, "but God," gave me the strength and peace I needed to make the right choice, which was to get out and stay out. Did I run? Yes, I ran.

> **"Now thanks be to God, who always leads us**
> **in triumph in Christ."**
> **2 Corinthians 2:14 NKJV**

We can't take our emotions and our desires lightly when they aren't managed by God. Why not? Because we see the risks and chances we take, when we allow our emotions and desires to dictate things for us.

5
Unhealthy Soul Ties

When you are connected to an individual who's breaking you down mentally, emotionally, physically, or in any aspect of life, you know deep down inside that you need to shake them off. Somehow, though, you find yourself painfully trapped, and you can't get out. It's called an unhealthy soul tie.

Unhealthy soul ties are formed through subtle operations. Not all of them are formed intentionally. There are times that the person is not aware of the pain they are inflicting onto the other person. However, there is a sure way God has given to us to discern pure motives and true intentions. We know Him as the Holy Spirit. He teaches us how to distinguish between good and bad. It is so important that we ask God to teach us how to discern intentions. We have a human nature, and that nature is flawed and full of weaknesses.

> **"The spirit is willing, but the flesh is weak."**
> **Matthew 26:41b NIV**

Our enemy, the devil, is very much aware of our human frailties, and certainly uses them to snare us by gaining access into our soul realm. Our soul consists of our mind where information is communicated, our ability to reason, our emotions, and our will. John 10:10 calls the devil a thief.

God only strips to build; the devil strips to kill. If there is no building or rebuilding taking place in any relationship we are in, this may be a sure indication that the relationship is not from God.

> **"Fulfil ye my joy, that ye be likeminded, having the same love, being of one accord, of one mind."**
> **Philippians 2:2**

At this present moment, there are new divorcees scratching their heads, wondering if it is just a dream and finding out it is not. Reality speaks volumes about how unclear the married couple was about the vows of marriage. On the flip side of the coin, there are marriages existing primary for one purpose and one purpose only: convenience!

I have pointed out phrases and statements quite a bit. This one, I must mention: "I wouldn't take that!" We say we won't take something, yet we kept on taking this and that. From the moment we come out of the womb, the enemy starts on all of us.

> **"For we wrestle not against flesh and blood, but against principalities, against powers, against the rulers of the darkness of this world..."**
> **Ephesian 6:12a**

No one is exempt. You would probably think that since children are little people and youths are young people, that they'd catch a break. Not so. Why? Because they also have what we all have in common as human beings—the five senses—vision, hearing, taste, touch, and smell.

Only God would have known, if He hadn't revealed it to us by His Spirit, that these five senses we take for granted every day, become weapons of mass destruction in the devil's hands. Our natural senses, in a spiritual sense, are open gateways to our souls. Satan uses these entrances to formulate seemingly unbreakable habits and addictive soul ties. There is so much more to these revelations than we even know.

> **"For it is a shame even to speak of those things which are done of them in secret."**
> **Ephesians 5:5**

> **"For I know that in me (that is, in my flesh) nothing good dwells."**
> **Romans 7:18a NKJV**

A little further on, in the book, I will unveil ways the devil uses our senses, and I will expose some of his devices.

Satan is very insidious and hard to detect without the Holy Spirit revealing him. In Hosea 4:6 NIV, God says, *"My people are destroyed from lack of knowledge."* As God unveils Satan's schemes, tricks, and cunning devices, we gain an advantage. *"Lest Satan should get an advantage of us: for we are not ignorant of his devices."* 2 Corinthians 2:11

As we learn how distorted views, wrong mind-sets, and wrong perceptions are formed, this makes us better gatekeepers over our five senses and over our children's open gateways.

If these gateways can be used to snare us, I can see why the Almighty wants us to give them to Him. We are admonished to present our bodies as a living sacrifice.

"I beseech you therefore, brethren, by the mercies of God, that ye present your bodies a living sacrifice, holy, acceptable unto God, which is your reasonable service."
Romans 12:1

The Holy Spirit also works through our senses and uses every one of them.

"Then laid they their hands on them, and they received the Holy Ghost."
Acts 8:17

"He who has an ear, let him hear what the Spirit says to the churches."
Revelation 2:7a NKJV

The more you read the Word of God, the more it becomes sweet like honey and you acquire a taste for it.

"O taste and see that the Lord is good; blessed is the man that trust[s] in Him."
Psalm 34:8

***"How sweet are Your words to my taste,
Sweeter than honey to my mouth!"
Psalm 119:103 NKJV***

***"…An odor of a sweet smell, a sacrifice
acceptable, well pleasing to God."
Philippians 4:18b***

***"For all that is in the world—the lust of the flesh,
the lust of the eyes, and the pride of life—
is not of the Father but is of the world."
1 John 2:16 NKJV***

Satan is a master deceiver with the use of words. He is a copycat of God that uses God's forum of communication, to conform us. *"Do not be conformed to this world, but be transformed by the renewing of your mind…" Romans 12:2a NKJV*

Over time, if harsh words are constantly spoken, these words become weights which hold enough power to reshape and frame your perception of yourself. This is called verbal abuse.

Mental abuse is like a massive cloud of confusion, and I feel it's the worst type of abuse. Am I in any way categorizing these types of abusive devices? Absolutely not, because one is no greater than the other. I personally feel that your mind is everything, and once you lose it, you've lost your will, your way, and all sense of empowerment and direction.

When a person is exerting physical strength against you, and causing bodily harm, the beating is meant to conform you to think and act differently than what the scripture teaches. *"For whom He did foreknow, He also did predestinate to be conformed to the image of His Son." Romans 8:29* However, if your view on love is distorted, you'll find yourself making excuses for the abuse, ultimately surrendering your self-worth.

"Do you not know that your body is the temple of the Holy Spirit?"
1 Corinthians 6:19a NKJV

An unhealthy sexual soul tie is formed when an individual knowingly uses the powerful tool of sex, as a means of mind control. You'll meet these people on the street, but it can also happen right in your own bedroom. Even in the union of marriage, if sex is used as a means for punishment or manipulation, this happens.

The Bible has some advice for married couples. *"The wife hath not power of her own body, but the husband: and likewise also the husband hath not power of his own body, but the wife. Defraud ye not one the other, except it be with consent for a time, that ye may give yourselves to fasting and prayer; and come together again, that Satan tempt you not for your incontinency." 1 Corinthians 7:4-5.* Anything other than this, is like an open door for infidelity with your consent on it.

Let's talk about mind games. There are some individuals whom intentionally manipulate relationships. No matter what the reason is, the underlining motive is for their own gain. They consider themselves amazingly skilled with their use of words, and gloat about what they are doing. When someone like this is in your life, your reasoning becomes baffled, and you think from a constant state of doubt and mistrust. Their aim is to always point the finger back at you.

"For God is not the author of confusion."
1 Corinthians 14:33

We all have a demon to fight, but it is worse for those of us who have people like this in our lives. They were assigned to look for our weaknesses. They came, not as a mistake, but to purposely turn lives upside down.

Here, I want to reference Paul's thorn in the flesh, only as a weakness, and not as an unhealthy soul tie. I want to demonstrate how Paul understood his need for God's help.

"Three times, I pleaded with the Lord
to take it away from me."
2 Corinthians 12:8 NIV

We do not know what Paul's weakness was, because there was no mention as to what it was. However, we do know that Paul asked the Lord three times to remove it.

We have a dire need for God's divine help in overcoming our continuously unbroken flow of questions and insecurities. We question if we are good enough. Sometimes these questions are compounded by a poor self-image and feelings of rejection that stems from unhealthy soul ties.

We all feel a need to belong, driving us to search for comfort, sometimes in all the wrong places. This happens when we choose to be validated by man rather than God.

I believe that after Adam fell, a void was left in all of us that only God can fill. That void exceeds any worldly or human capacity. It was never God's will for us to lose our place of security, or our sense of belonging.

> ***"For as by one man's disobedience many were made sinners, so by the obedience of one shall many be made righteous."***
> ***Romans 5:19***

God is just, and He did not leave us in a fallen state. Amen!

6

The Waiting Process

The waiting process is just that; it's a process of waiting and completing the actions given to us by God, to achieve an end. As He takes us through it, we need to stay focused, determined, true to change, and recognize when we are distracted from our purpose. Keep your determination, because God's timing is not yours.

"Beloved, be not ignorant of this one thing,
that one day is with the Lord as a thousand years
and a thousand years as one day."
2 Peter 3:8

Determination gives you a strong desire to see the end. It strengthens your love for God and helps you through the waiting process.

"Take My yoke upon you and learn from Me,
for I am gentle and lowly in heart,
and you will find rest for your souls.
For My yoke is easy, and my burden is light."
Matthew 11:29-30 NKJV

The waiting process is where the refining takes place. As you read the Word of God, it starts tearing down the enemy's well-fortified strongholds that were built through the imagination of lies. These lies exalt themselves against the truth of God's spoken word. They are anything contrary to what God says about you.

"Casting down imaginations, and every high
thing that exalts itself against the knowledge of
God, and bringing into captivity every thought
to the obedience of Christ."
2 Corinthians 10:5

"Therefore, if anyone is in Christ, the new creation
has come: The old has gone, the new is here!"
2 Corinthians 5:17 NIV

God assures us of His finished work on the cross, *"Having reconciled us back to himself." 2 Corinthians 5:19.* Because of the blood of His Son, Jesus, we have victory.

He teaches us the mysteries of the Kingdom of Heaven (Matthew 13:11). We learn the true, unconditional love of a Heavenly Father who is full of grace, mercy, and truth.

**"God so loved the world, that He gave
His only begotten Son."
John 3:16a**

And we also have an inheritance, which He has given to us. (Roman 8:17, Galatians 3:29)

**"God sent not his son into the world
to condemn the world; but that the world
through him might be saved."
John 3:17**

**"If we confess our sins, He is faithful and just to
forgive us our sins, and to cleanse us
from all unrighteousness."
1 John 1:9**

Through this waiting process, not only is God refining us, but He is also preparing those who are chosen for the ministry of marriage. Depending on the calling and God's plan, the timing for the process can differ. Loneliness and discouragement will come. You may even think it is impossible to wait. But we gain wisdom from His wisdom. He builds Godly character into us as He teaches us what it means to *"Fight the good fight of the faith." 1 Timothy 6:12 NIV*

God, by His wisdom alone, creates a thirst in us to want more of Him. By His wisdom and His understanding, we become skilled masters at whatever task He gives us.

> ***"So give your servant a discerning heart
> to govern your people and to distinguish
> between right and wrong."***
> ***1 Kings 3:9a NIV***

> ***"Happy is the man [or woman]
> who finds wisdom, and the man [or woman]
> who gains understanding."***
> ***Proverbs 3:13 NKJV***

When God opens our understanding, it gives us opportunities to assess situations from His perspective. God will use this training ground to develop spiritual fruit in you. He teaches us that there is a more excellent way to love. As a single parent in this process, I can testify to this.

> ***"And now abide faith, hope, love, these three;
> but the greatest of these is love."***
> ***1 Corinthians 13:13 NKJV***

We never stop growing in God, and God is consistent with perfecting our love. We learn self-control. Pride is crushed, as we take on humility. He puts an unfeigned, sincere "yes" in our soul, and doing His will becomes a delight.

> ***"Then you will find your joy in the Lord,
> and I will cause you to ride in triumph on
> the heights of the land, and to feast on the
> inheritance of your father, Jacob:
> for the mouth of the Lord has spoken."***
> ***Isaiah 58:14 NIV***

The greatest gift that is developed in this waiting process is our love for God. It becomes our driving force and the reason for everything we do. As you embark on this new journey, you stand to gain so much in this waiting process. You will even gain a reintroduction to the new and confident you.

7
Submission

Upon accepting Jesus Christ as our Lord and Savior on a personal level, we learn submission to God. It becomes an important factor in our walk with God. It's not something that we're automatically born to do.

"I was shape[d] in iniquity;
and in sin did my mother conceive me."
Psalm 51:5

"For there is not a just man upon the earth
who does good and does not sin."
Ecclesiastes 7:20 NKJV

Through us choosing to remain consistent in prayer, and studying His Word, God builds our faith and trust in Himself. *"So then faith comes by hearing, and hearing by the Word of God." Romans 10:17 NKJV*

This faith pushes us to a course of actions. We resist and submit. *"Submit yourselves therefore to God. Resist the devil, and he will flee from you." James 4:7 ESV*

It sounds easy, but it can be difficult. It involves breaking our own agenda of thoughts, feelings, actions, conducts, and attitudes. God showed his patience to us through His Son, Jesus Christ. He has demonstrated what it means to be "longsuffering toward us." He really does wait on each of us, individually.

We can be stubborn, rebellious, self-righteousness, judgmental, and critical. We are often self-consumed, indulging only in what we believe is right. The list doesn't stop there. Sometimes a desire to submit is there, and we want to do what is right, but some strongholds in our personality oppose His will. I see them as the dominate and strongest sides of ourselves, that tend to oppose Him.

These strongholds are sometimes not easily broken, yet He still waits on us. As we align ourselves with His will, we can easily confess, "God, Your way is right." God has provided a way of escape, for us to overcome whatever is blocking us from surrendering to Him.

"Is not my word like fire? declares the Lord, and like a hammer that breaks a rock in pieces?"
Jeremiah 23:29 NIV

"The word of God is quick, and powerful, and sharper than any two-edged sword, piercing even to the dividing asunder of soul and spirit, and of the joints and marrow, and is a discerner of the thoughts and intents of the heart."
Hebrew 4:12

What a mighty God we serve! Oh, what a blessing it is to know that even when we are in a negative state of mind, God, through His Word, reaches us right where we are.

"Surely the arm of the Lord is not too short to save, nor his ear too dull to hear."
Isaiah 59:1 NIV

No matter why we are in a negative place, there is always a cause and an effect. But to know that no place is too far for God to reach us, is more wonderful than words can express.

8

Don't Stay Stuck in Reverse

When we continue to repeat patterns and get stuck in reverse, it hinders our full potential and keeps us from evolving into what God has called us to be. We can never move forward in the direction God is taking us, by looking backwards.

"You have been wandering around in this hill country long enough; turn to the north."
Deuteronomy 2:3 NLT

Here is an awesome analogy about how we look when God is calling us to move forward, yet we are motionless. When a car's transmission is going out, if the gear is stuck in forward, the car may jump or even rock, but one thing is certain, it's going nowhere.

God does expect us to move at some point in time. Does he condemn us when we are stuck? No! But we do not want to set someone or something up as a fallback, or as comfort cushions, and exalt them over God, rather than moving forward.

> ***"I am the Lord: that is My name;***
> ***and My glory will I not give to another,***
> ***neither My praise to graven images."***
> ***Isaiah 42:8***

It is important to recognize at what point you are relapsing. Is it the same place every time? Once you recognize that place, it's just as important to learn what God is developing in you, and what He is working out of you.

Satan is adamant about stopping destiny. God is adamant about helping us to break our cycles of negative patterns. Remember, just as the angels of God fight on our behalf, the devil has a will and fights against us.

I'll leave you with this question: What are you going to do about your repeated patterns?

If a guy makes an approach, here are some things to keep in mind:

- Don't appear desperate.

- Don't jump from zero to one hundred.

- Keep your focus and know what you want.

- Don't be disappointed if he doesn't call back.

- Don't be in it alone; know when he's no longer interested.

- Don't blame yourself.

- Avoid feelings of rejection.

- If he's not the one, learn to be okay with it.

- Allow him to have a free will.

- Give your emotions to God.

Notes

Notes

Notes

Notes

Notes

53

Notes

Notes

Notes

P.O. Box 453
Powder Springs, Georgia 30127
770.727.6517

info@entegritypublishing.com
www.entegritypublishing.com